CHICKEN RUN ™

Storybook

Adapted by Terry Collins

Screenplay by Karey Kirkpatrick
Story by Peter Lord and Nick Park
Directed by Peter Lord and Nick Park
Produced by Peter Lord, David Sproxton and

TM & © 2000 DreamWorks LLC, Aardman Chicken Run Limited and Pathé Image.
Landoll, Inc. Ashland, Ohio 44805
Made in Canada.
07357-1678

Ginger, leader of the hens of Tweedy's Farm, was a chicken with a mission. Her goal? To free herself and all her feathered friends from egg-laying captivity! Using a spoon as part of her latest scheme, she dug under the fence to freedom.

The first one to crawl through was Bunty, but then—disaster! Bunty's bottom was too big. "Ginger, help! I'm stuck!" she cried.

Ginger always knew that escaping wasn't going to be easy. . . .

"No chicken escapes from Tweedy's Farm!" Mr. Tweedy said as he tossed Ginger into the coal bin for the tenth time.

Ginger glared back. She knew Mr. Tweedy would have to let her out eventually, and then . . . she would try *again*.

After locking Ginger away, Mr. Tweedy stepped into the house. "Those chickens are organized, I know it!" he muttered.

"No, it's all in your head," Mrs. Tweedy said, correcting her husband. "Those chickens just aren't laying enough eggs. We're getting out of the egg business. I've found a way to make us some *real* money!"

Days later, Mr. Tweedy returned Ginger to Hut 17.

"Morning, Ginger," Babs said brightly, knitting. "Back from holiday?"

Not everyone was as cheerful as Babs. After dozens of failed attempts, they were ready to give up trying to escape. But Ginger was determined. "We can't just give up!" she said. "There's a whole world out there. I mean—freedom."

When the other chickens still looked skeptical, Ginger stepped outside and sighed. "Heaven, help us."

Suddenly, from out of nowhere, a rooster crash-landed in the chicken feeder!

A torn circus poster fluttered down into Ginger's hands. "Rocky the Flying Rooster," she read aloud.

"That's me," the dazed rooster replied.

"You're the answer!" a newly   inspired Ginger cried. "We'll *fly* out of here!"

A brightly decorated truck pulled up outside the coop.
"The circus!" Rocky cried. "They've found me!"
"Teach us chickens how to fly and we'll hide you,"
Ginger pleaded.
Rocky tried to protest, but Ginger remained firm.
"Okay," he reluctantly agreed. "We'll start tomorrow."

The next day, Rocky put the hens to work. Jumping jacks. Wing whips. Fanny fluffs. Ginger confronted Rocky with her doubts.

"There a problem, doll face?" he asked from the comfort of his hot tub.

"The name's Ginger," she corrected. "And I thought you were going to teach us how to fly."

"Hey, do I tell you how to lay eggs?" Rocky replied. "Relax, we're making progress."

Ginger snorted. Was the arrogant rooster *really* teaching them anything?

"What you hens need is thrust," Rocky announced, pulling tight a pair of suspenders scavenged by the barnyard rats, Nick and Fetcher.

A nervous Bunty sat on the launching pad.

"Release!" Rocky cried, and the hefty hen shot into the air!

"Poultry in motion!" Nick heckled . . . until Bunty crashed headfirst into the fence.

The chickens were beginning to lose hope.

A few days later, a special delivery arrived for the Tweedys.

"What is it?" Mr. Tweedy wondered as he unpacked a box of machine parts.

"Our future," Mrs. Tweedy said with an evil smile. "This device will make us rich, taking our farm out of the dark ages and into full . . . scale . . . automated . . . production."

That night, Rocky wanted to boost the chickens' spirits, so he turned on a radio and started to dance! "It's called rhythm, and you can't fly without it!" he crowed.

All the chickens began to dance along—except for one. Ginger thought the exercise was silly . . . until Rocky spun her on the floor.

She had to admit—he *was* quite dashing. And now that his wing had healed from his crash-landing, perhaps he could *show* them how to fly! That would lift their spirits.

Suddenly, Mr. Tweedy's guard dog appeared, backing Ginger into the farmer's waiting hand. He took Ginger into the barn and clamped her onto the conveyor belt of the strange-looking pie machine he'd built.

"Chickens go in—pies come out," Mrs. Tweedy sneered as she pressed the start button.

Luckily for Ginger, Rocky had followed her into the barn. He would save her!

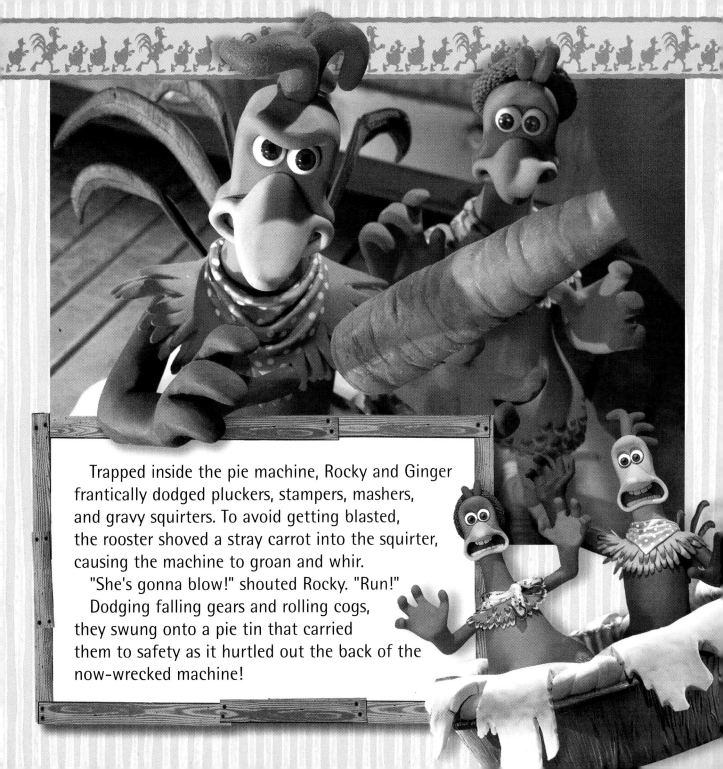

   Trapped inside the pie machine, Rocky and Ginger
frantically dodged pluckers, stampers, mashers,
and gravy squirters. To avoid getting blasted,
the rooster shoved a stray carrot into the squirter,
causing the machine to groan and whir.
   "She's gonna blow!" shouted Rocky. "Run!"
   Dodging falling gears and rolling cogs,
they swung onto a pie tin that carried
them to safety as it hurtled out the back of the
now-wrecked machine!

Returning to Hut 17, Ginger told the others about the pie machine.

"I don't want to be a pie! I don't like gravy!" Babs squawked in terror.

"Ladies, please. Rocky sabotaged the machine!" Ginger said confidently. "And he's going to fly for us tomorrow!"

However, Rocky wasn't so sure. Hanging his head, he crept outside.

Later that night, Ginger joined Rocky on the roof. "Thank you," she said, "for saving my life."

Together, they looked towards the hill in the distance.

"I come up here every night and imagine what it must be like over there," Ginger said.

"Yeah, well, um . . . life, you know, it can be full of disappointments," Rocky replied sadly. Despite all of his bragging, even *he* knew that chickens couldn't fly! What was he going to do?

The next morning when Ginger came to get Rocky for his flying demonstration, the rooster was gone—leaving behind nothing but the bottom half of his circus poster.

"Shot out of a cannon," Ginger said. "That's how he flew!"

All of the chickens began arguing until Fowler, a mascot of the Royal Air Force, stepped forward. "Quiet in the ranks," he commanded. "A squad must work together. That's how you win medals."

A beam of sunlight gleamed off Fowler's RAF medal and caught Ginger's eye.

"That's it!" Ginger cried. "We're still going to fly out of here!"

The chickens were filled with new hope. They began hurriedly constructing a flying machine from the wood of their own coops. Nick and Fetcher provided other needed materials—even Christmas lights for a runway.

Sawing, hammering, adjusting—they raced against the clock, until a loud engine noise came sputtering from the barn.

"Mr. Tweedy's fixed the pie machine!" Babs cried.

"Then we're escaping!" Ginger said. "Now!"

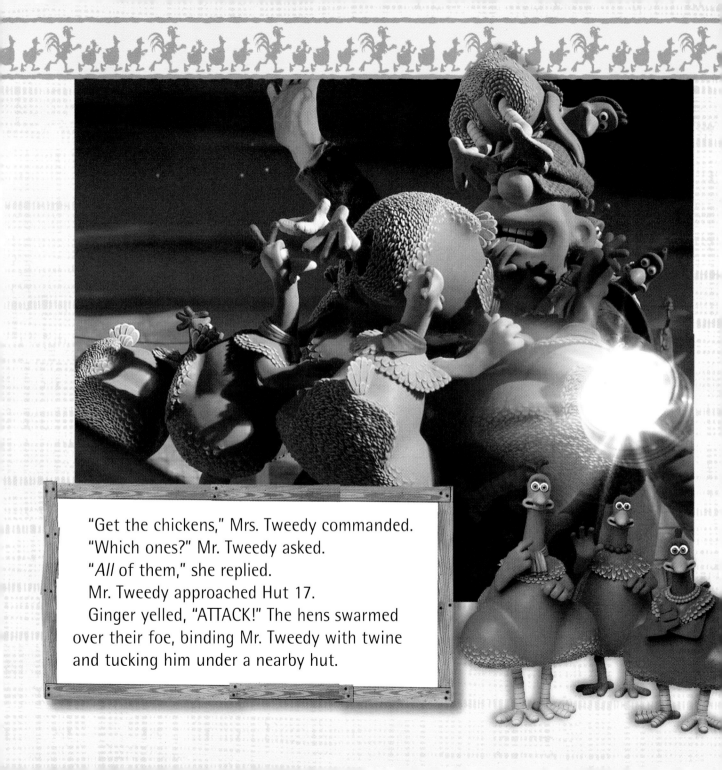

"Get the chickens," Mrs. Tweedy commanded.

"Which ones?" Mr. Tweedy asked.

"*All* of them," she replied.

Mr. Tweedy approached Hut 17.

Ginger yelled, "ATTACK!" The hens swarmed over their foe, binding Mr. Tweedy with twine and tucking him under a nearby hut.

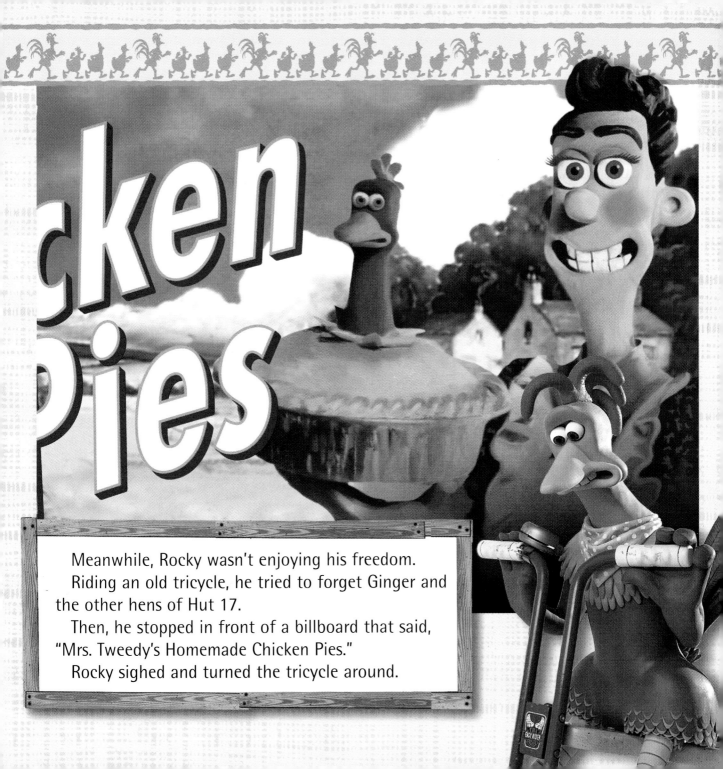

Meanwhile, Rocky wasn't enjoying his freedom.

Riding an old tricycle, he tried to forget Ginger and the other hens of Hut 17.

Then, he stopped in front of a billboard that said, "Mrs. Tweedy's Homemade Chicken Pies."

Rocky sighed and turned the tricycle around.

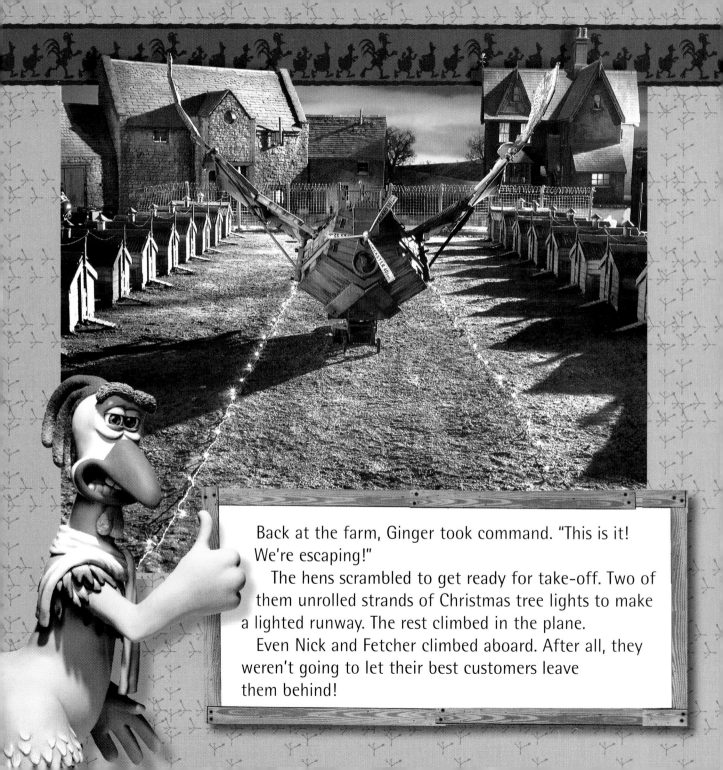

Back at the farm, Ginger took command. "This is it! We're escaping!"

The hens scrambled to get ready for take-off. Two of them unrolled strands of Christmas tree lights to make a lighted runway. The rest climbed in the plane.

Even Nick and Fetcher climbed aboard. After all, they weren't going to let their best customers leave them behind!

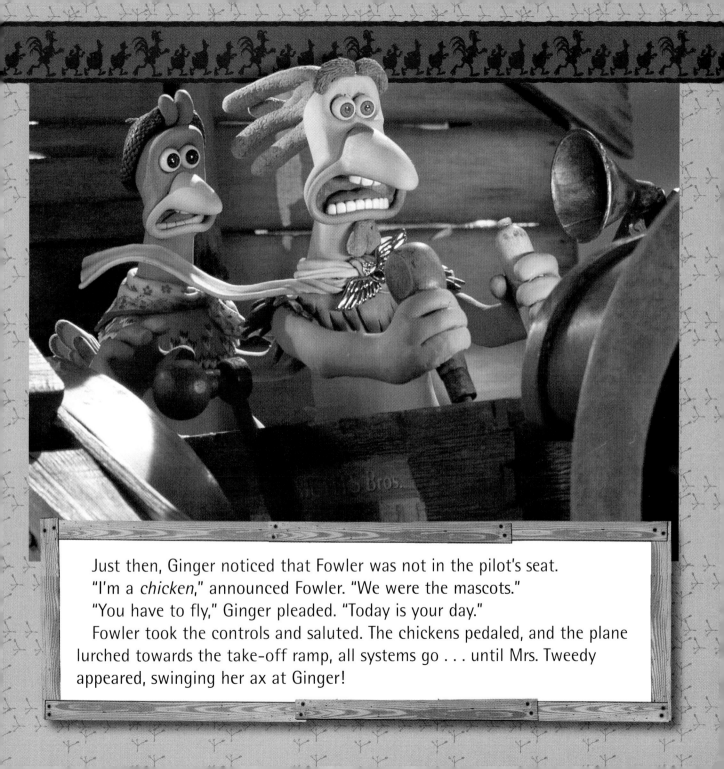

Just then, Ginger noticed that Fowler was not in the pilot's seat.

"I'm a *chicken*," announced Fowler. "We were the mascots."

"You have to fly," Ginger pleaded. "Today is your day."

Fowler took the controls and saluted. The chickens pedaled, and the plane lurched towards the take-off ramp, all systems go . . . until Mrs. Tweedy appeared, swinging her ax at Ginger!

But Rocky returned just in time.

"Gingerrrrr!" he called, as he flew over the fence on his tricycle knocking Mrs. Tweedy to the ground.

As the plane took off, Rocky and Ginger saw a strand of lights dangling from the plane. With a lunge, they grabbed the lights and climbed aboard.

Unfortunately, Mrs. Tweedy had also grabbed the lights!

Ax in hand, Mrs. Tweedy climbed toward the plane. Scissors in hand, Ginger went down to meet her. As Mrs. Tweedy swung the ax, Ginger ducked, and Mrs. Tweedy sliced through the lights.

Mrs. Tweedy fell . . . landing right in the pie machine. Steam hissed. Gears churned. And with a mighty WHA-BOOM, a mushroom cloud of gravy exploded!

"I told you they was organized," said Mr. Tweedy, as the plane soared towards the setting sun.

"Is it as good as you imagined?" asked Rocky the next day, as they looked out at their new home. It was nestled safely inside a protected bird sanctuary.

Ginger ran her toes through the cool, green grass.

There were no fences or farmers here. The chickens were free at last.

Ginger grabbed Rocky's hand and smiled. "Better," she said.